Counting with Office Supplies!

By Malcolm Shealy

Illustrated by Meg Dunn

 A GOLDEN BOOK • NEW YORK

Published in the United States by Golden Books, an imprint of Random House Children's Books, a division of Penguin
Random House LLC, 1745 Broadway, New York, NY 10019, and in Canada by Penguin Random House Canada Limited,
Toronto. Golden Books, A Golden Book, A Little Golden Book, the G colophon, and the distinctive gold spine are registered
trademarks of Penguin Random House LLC.
rhcbooks.com
Educators and librarians, for a variety of teaching tools, visit us at RHTeachersLibrarians.com
ISBN 978-0-593-48295-7 (trade) — ISBN 978-0-593-48296-4 (ebook)
Printed in the United States of America
10 9 8 7 6 5 4 3

Dunder Mifflin Paper Company

is a very busy place. Michael, Pam, Jim, Dwight, and their co-workers need all kinds of supplies to keep the office running smoothly.

2

TWO pens, both out of ink.
Oh, Andy. . . .

3

Three colorful folders . . .
Michael just can't decide.

Five extra invitations
to the big office birthday party.
Phyllis doesn't want to leave anyone out.

7

Seven beets in the break room refrigerator are the ultimate office snack.

Eight sticky notes remind everyone
of an important office meeting . . .

9

. . . but **nine** rolls of tape keep
the meeting room shut!
(Where's Michael?)

Ten doughnuts . . .
who brings only ten doughnuts?
(Poor Toby.)

Just kidding! A good manager makes sure
there are doughnuts for everyone in the office!